Hide and Seek

First published in 2009
by Wayland

Text copyright © Anna Matthew 2009
Illustration copyright © Heather Heyworth 2009

Wayland
338 Euston Road
London NW1 3BH

Wayland Australia
Level 17/207 Kent Street
Sydney, NSW 2000

Series Editor: Louise John
Editor: Katie Powell
Cover design: Paul Cherrill
Design: D.R.ink
Consultant: Shirley Bickler

A CIP catalogue record for this book is available from the British Library.

ISBN 9780750259262

Printed in China

Wayland is a division of Hachette Children's Books,
an Hachette UK Company

www.hachette.co.uk

Hide and Seek

Written by Anna Matthew
Illustrated by Heather Heyworth

WAYLAND

We are playing
hide and seek.

I am IT.

5

Look out!

I am coming to find you.

7

I can see feet in the shed.

Come out! I can see you.

I can see a head
in the flowers.

Look out!

I am coming to get you.

I can see you up
in the tree.

You cannot hide
from me!

13

Look out!

I am coming to find you
in the flowerpot!

I can see fingers
on the bin.

Come out! You cannot
hide from me!

17

Look! Boots under
the gate!

Come out!

I can see you.

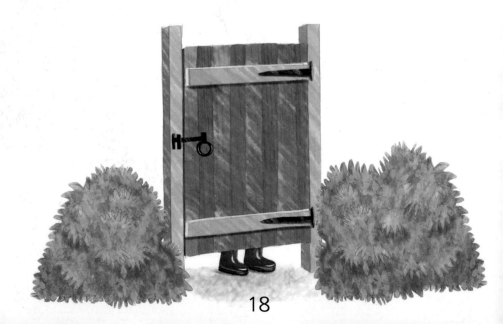

18

No, you cannot see me.

Here I am!

I am
IT now!

Guiding a First Read of
Hide and Seek

It is important to talk through the book with the child before they read it alone. This prepares them for the way the story unfolds, and allows them to enjoy the pictures as you both talk naturally, using the language they will later encounter when reading. Read them the brief overview below, and then follow the suggestions:

1. Talking through the book

The girl is telling us about a game of Hide and Seek. She is IT and when she looks carefully, she can see parts of the children who are hiding.

Let's read the title: **Hide and Seek**
Turn to page 4. The girl says, "I am IT."
What is she doing in the picture?
Now turn over.
"Look out," she says. "I am coming to find you."
What can she see in the shed on page 8? Yes, feet.
On the next page, she can see a head in
the flowers.

Continue through the book, guiding the discussion to fit the text as the child looks at the illustrations.

On the last page, was she right about the boots?
No! The boy is talking now, and he says, "No, you can't see me. Here I am!"

2. A first reading of the book

Ask the child to read the book independently, pointing carefully underneath each word (tracking), while thinking about the story. Praise attempts by the child to correct themselves, and prompt them to use their letter knowledge, the punctuation and check the meaning, for example:

"I can see shoes in the shed." Yes, that makes sense, but what letter does 'shoes' start with? Try it again, and check the letters. Well done.

Yes, 'hat' starts with 'h'. Now check the last letter. What else would make sense? "Is it head?" Good, you checked the word carefully.

3. Follow-up activities

The high frequency words in this title are:

a   am   are   can   come   I   in   look   out   see the   to   you

- Select two high frequency words, and ask the child to find them throughout the book. Discuss the shape of the letters and their letter sounds.
- To memorise the words, ask the child to write them in the air, then write them repeatedly on a whiteboard or on paper, leaving a space between each attempt.

4. Encourage

- Reading the book again – with expression.
- Drawing a picture based on the story.
- Writing one or two sentences using the practised words.

START READING is a series of highly enjoyable books for beginner readers. **The books have been carefully graded to match the Book Bands widely used in schools.** This enables readers to be sure they choose books that match their own reading ability.

Look out for the Band colour on the book in our Start Reading logo.

The Bands are:

Pink Band 1A & 1B

Red Band 2

Yellow Band 3

Blue Band 4

Green Band 5

Orange Band 6

Turquoise Band 7

Purple Band 8

Gold Band 9

START READING books can be read independently or shared with an adult. They promote the enjoyment of reading through satisfying stories supported by fun illustrations.

Anna Matthew loves writing stories about when she was a child. She lived in a seaside town and spent lots of time playing on the beach, and in the park and street. Now her two children are growing up, and she can write about their fun and games, too!

Heather Heyworth lives in Suffolk with her husband, two children and a very demanding cat called Wooster!